THE ADVENTURE OF THE PRINCE

Copyright, 2021 Aasir Diab

All rights reserved.

DEDICATION

To both my Grandpas;

May they rest in peace.

CONTENTS

Chapter 1 - Pg. 3

Chapter 2 - Pg. 5

Chapter 3 - Pg. 9

Chapter 4 - Pg. 13

Chapter 5 - Pg. 17

Chapter 6 - Pg. 21

Chapter 7 - Pg. 24

Chapter 8 - Pg. 27

Chapter 9 - Pg. 30

Chapter 10 - Pg. 32

Chapter 11 - Pg. 36

Chapter 12 - Pg. 40

Chapter 13 - Pg. 44

Chapter 14 - Pg. 49

Chapter 15 - Pg. 52

Chapter 16 - Pg. 55

Chapter 17 - Pg. 59

Chapter 18 - Pg. 61

Chapter 19 - Pg. 64

Chapter 20 - Pg. 66

Chapter 1
I Hate Being a Prince

The chapter title doesn't sound too believable, right? Yeah, I really should get that fixed. Anyway, it's true. I really do hate being a prince. You're probably thinking, "Well, why do you hate being a prince?"; and I wouldn't blame you. I mean, people in the village basically worship you and your parents. You also practically get anything you want.

But you know why I hate it? It was because of my Dad

My Dad is a fat slob, which I guess is a bit harsh, but you would know what I mean if you had lived with him 24/7. He's always got some sort of food with him, and his ego is bigger than his belly. Another thing about me hating being a prince is that I have a goofy name. Ready for it? It's...

...Benkieus Underman Maplet III.

Yeah, yeah, get your chuckles in. You can stop anytime now. Okay, seriously, it's not that funny.

STOP!!!!

Sorry, I just go ballistic at the talk of my name (It almost as if the author of this book just pressed random letters). People call me Ben for short, which is a better name than Benkieus. I also never understood the "III" part. Why do people need to know that I'm related to some dead people? It seems completely unnecessary.

I also hate my initials. I'm not spelling them out, as it's obvious what it is. If you're laughing right now (AGAIN!!!!!), then I hate you.

Okay, okay, I don't.

But stop laughing at my name.

STOP!!!!

Chapter 2
My Dad's Obsession

So, now that you know about my stupid name and my stupid life, I guess you should get to know my family more. My Dad is obsessed (and I mean OBSESSED) with dragons. Not like cartoon ones, but real ones. We have tons of crossbows and swords stashed in our castle, ready for battle, but Dad just doesn't know how to capture a dragon.

So now you're probably like," Why is your Dad trying to capture a dragon??! Is he a crazy lunatic??!!"

No.

Well, he is a crazy lunatic, but that's not the reason he's trying to catch dragons.

It's all because of my Mom.

No, my Mom hasn't passed, but it's kind of hard to explain. She's currently standing in my Dad's bedroom, rock-solid, because she's made of diamond.

Let me rephrase that.

She turned into a diamond.

It happened because someone showed up at the castle one day, and his name was Midas Diamond Touch. Weird name, right? Anyway, I opened my mouth to ask a question, but he cut me off and said, "Yes, I know it's Midas Golden Touch. That's my brother!!" I was going to ask him why his name was so weird, but I just kept my mouth shut.

He then demanded, "Where is Queen Bena??" (My Mom). My Dad shouted back, "None of your goddamn beeswax!!!" So, Midas went to find her himself, walking past my Dad, before touching him and turning him into pure diamond. As Midas walked into my parent's room, I heard my Mom's voice. "We meet again, old friend".

The last thing I remember was my Mom reaching her hand out towards me before she began to fade into a blueish colour. She then turned into a solid diamond right before my eyes.

By now, you're probably thinking, " how did your dad turn back into a human?" The only cure to the spell of turning a diamond back into a human is a single drop of dragon's blood. We thought it would be impossible to get, but I found a jar behind a dusty set of books in our brewing room.

The choice was hard. Do I bring back Mom? Or Dad? I was going to go for my Mom, but I tripped, and the jar smashed over my Dad, exposing the dragon's blood to his diamond skin. However, instead of thanking me, you know what he does? He shouts at me! He tells me why I couldn't have freed him sooner.

I couldn't take it anymore; that night, I slept in the courtyard on a pile of hay because I just couldn't stand being with him in that castle for the rest of the day. He also hates when other people disagree with him. Once, he asked one of our knights what his favourite sandwich was. The knight said fish paste and sausage. This was the wrong answer. Before you could say, "cheese and fish paste with onions and sausages", the knight's head was now home to a brand-new shiny pole.

Chapter 3
A Missed Chance

Now you know that for now, until my Dad captures a dragon and retrieves a drop of its blood, Mom will sit, cold and blue-faced, in my Dad's room. I still haven't forgiven Dad, and he'll probably remain a big, fat, lazy bum who does nothing but shout orders at people and eat.

Another thing about my Dad: He's an extreme cheapskate!!! He says I must "deal with the olden times", to which I responded, "Doesn't the olden times mean being a fat guy that dreams about chicken every night in his underwear?" Yeah, that one got me grounded for a week.

Anyways, right now, Dad is rambling on and on about how he's really going to catch a dragon; but I'm barely listening because I know it's never going to happen. He says the same thing every few days. However, this time, he did say something different that he would bait it with blueberries.

That's extremely dangerous. I've read in an old dusty dragon history book that dragons can smell blueberries from miles away. So, when Dad got out a big basket of blueberries and placed them in the courtyard, I started to get worried.

Then, something strange began to happen. Smoke filled the sky. I was coughing like crazy. And to my surprise, a real dragon popped his head into the courtyard! It swooshed around, breathing flames. Dad was desperately trying to extinguish the fires using my prince cape!! Grr...

Anyway, the knights raised their crossbows. They shot..., and they missed!! Nice shot, guys...

Eventually, they got smart and threw up a giant net, and the dragon was pulled to the ground, just as it was scrambling to get off the ground. We had a dragon in the courtyard!! I don't think that's ever happened before.

Dad walked right up to it and said with wide eyes, "I caught a dragon!!" (His words, not mine.) He was still amazed, staring at it. The whole time I was thinking, "JUST GET THE DAMN BLOOD!!"

FINALLY, Dad gets out a little knife and cuts a teeny-tiny slit in the dragon's arm. It roared loudly and sounded hurt, which is surprising for such a big guy. Blood drips down his arm, and Dad gets a drop of it in a jar. So now I'm like, "THIS IS FINALLY IT!!!!!!"

As Dad walked over to the castle, that's when the dragon decides to make its move. It suddenly broke free, and using its tail, slapped my Dad across the back and sent him crashing down to the ground, along with the drop of dragon blood. Dad's fine, but I wish I could say the same for the jar.

It smashed into bits and pieces, and just when we thought things couldn't get worse, they did.

The dragon flew away and escaped!

Chapter 4
Sadness Over the Kingdom

The next day, in the aftermath of yesterday's complete failure, Dad went into a big slump. He wouldn't get out of bed until the afternoon and didn't care what anyone in the castle was doing. The only thing he did was eat, like a lot, and way more than he used to before.

I, on the other hand, had something else on my mind. It was something that was completely unrelated to my Dad's slump and diamond Mom. I suspect that someone in the castle was a traitor who has lots of acquaintances with the dark arts. He has his own room, filled with strange and weird stuff. His name's Vodlif, and he always wears a dark robe, and I'm pretty sure he has a third eye or something because he never takes off his hood.

Once, I saw him quickly dash to his room, carrying a gun-shaped object in his hand. So, I'm pretty sure that's what it is. He's a mysterious character and likes to keep to himself but always shows up to gatherings and stuff.

I've never really gotten along with him very well, and he doesn't really like me either. My suspicions conclude that he's probably trying to take over the kingdom. And he knows the way to do this is by getting rid of my Dad and me because if my Dad's gone, I'll be king. And if I'm gone, no one can be king/queen because I have no brothers or sisters. Which probably makes it easier for him.

Now that I think about it, I know how the dragon escaped! I remember Vodlif creeping up ever so quietly and undoing the net, all while remaining mostly out of sight.

By doing this, Vodlif triggered the dragon's escape to freedom. That piece of crap!!! He knew that if Mom turned back into a human, he would have to deal with her as well.

I raced to my Dad's room. Rats! It's locked. I frantically banged on the door. Open up, open up, open up... please!!! "Please go away." my Dad managed to groan out. In defeat, I just walked away. I guess I'll tell him later. He's got to go to the bathroom or something at some point.

I spent the rest of the day spying on Vodlif. I was making sure he wasn't doing anything that looked suspicious. Eventually, Vodlif went into his room and shut the door. It seemed like he has something to hide.

The door was locked uptight. I couldn't resist not taking a quick look in there. My room was right next to Vodlif's, and there was a thin ledge that ran along the edge of the castle walls. It went around the entire backside of the structure. Quietly, I carefully slipped out of my window and shifted, inch by inch, hugging the wall towards Vodlif's room.

Below me was water, as the castle was built on suspended land over a massive chunk of water. I didn't really feel like swimming, so I just tried to stay as close to the wall as I could. I reached Vodlif's window, which was just low enough for me to peer inside. I saw Vodlif speaking with an executioner. In fact, he was the only executer in our town.

This was the Middle Ages. People have NO mercy. Anyways, I couldn't quite hear what they were yapping about, but I could mouth out their words. Kill..gold..the king...

I KNEW IT!! From what I could understand, Vodlif was paying the executer a huge sum of gold as a reward in exchange for killing the King "soon." (Soon isn't that far away.) I need to warn my Dad IMMEDIATELY!!!!!

I sneakily trudged back to my window, and as I'm about to climb back in, Vodlif comes into my room.

Oh, crap.

Chapter 5
The Preparation

Every book has that one boring chapter, right? Well, this is probably going to be it. I didn't do much today or for a few days because I was grounded. Yeah, I was grounded! After Vodlif caught me red-handed, he went and squealed to my Dad. That rat!

 I wanted to punch something. I wanted to punch everything. Heck, I wanted to punch the entire world. Dad was punishing me for something that was going to save his life!!!!!! Notice how I put "was." I'm not going to tell him anymore. He can fight his own battles.

Okay, okay, I'm not actually going to leave him in the dust, but I had to get more information on precisely what Vodlif was planning. The one thing I was certain about was that Vodlif couldn't be trusted.

So, I came up with a plan. Dad gave me some coins and sent me out to get food. Big surprise. Anyways, this was PERFECT because part of my plan involved getting out of the castle. (I was grounded, so I couldn't leave the castle, duh!)

I went and picked out the food that Dad wanted. On the way back to the castle, I went into Old Willy's Bar, which was, as you guessed it, a bar. I picked up a bottle of something called Knock-Out Zzz's. That night, I waited until Dad came in and said goodnight.

After a few minutes, I climbed out the window and shimmied my way back to Vodlif's room. As I peeked in the room, I could see the coast was clear. I assumed Vodlif could return to his room at any time to hit the hay any minute now; so, I had to act fast.

I tried to pull myself up to see better, but it was quite a high window. Okay, I'm getting there...

SLIP!

I slipped on some pebbles on the ledge. I was dangling over the edge of the ledge. Come on... come on... YES! I pulled myself back up onto the ledge, then tripped and landed headfirst into Vodlif's room. A glass of water was placed atop his dresser, so I seized the opportunity and spilled a few drops into the glass—one more for good luck. And with that, I crawled back into my window and had a good night's sleep.

I went straight into plan mode the next day. I knew that Vodlif was knocked out in his room right now. I also knew that Dad would be shouting Vodlif's name soon. So, the plan was still in action. Last night was only Phrase one. This was the second part.

I tiptoed into the kitchen, quiet as a mouse. I grabbed a knife. Then, quietly going back to the room, I held the knife over Vodlif. WAIT!! WHAT AM I DOING?? I can't kill him! There must be a better way. Killing him is crossing the line. Think, think! Just then, I heard a sound.

Dad was coming into Vodlif's room.

Chapter 6
The Untold Secrets

NO!!!! This was not part of the plan. I couldn't move Vodlif out of the way in time, so I had to save myself now (Sorry, not sorry, Vodlif). I concealed myself next to a bookshelf that was behind the door. I sucked in my breath, trying to hide as much of myself as possible. I was dead meat.

I'm dead meat. I'm dead meat. I'm dead meat. I'm dead me-

AHHHHHH!

The bookshelf flipped around, revealing a secret passageway. Unfortunately, I fell

down a flight of stairs, bumping my head on each step. When the stairs finally ended, I took a nasty fall to the ribs. Ow! I was in revolting pain.

If there's one good thing that came out of this, it's that Dad didn't spot me. But what do I do? I can try to crawl up the stairs to nurse myself up and-

No.

I can't! If Dad knows I was snooping around, then I would really be in trouble. I might as well look around. When my eyes adjusted to the darkness, I could see rows of what looked like ancient writing on the wall, lots of cobwebs, and dust. There was also a box of old books. This place really needed a spring clean. Anyway, these books were written in some fancy old-timey language. I couldn't understand a word. Then, the unspeakable happened. The letters began to move around all by themselves!

They started glowing a bring, luminous yellow and were grabbing at me! I was almost sucked into the book. Luckily, I closed right at the last second. Phew, I'm not touching that book again. I jumped on the book like a small trampoline, just to be on the safe side.

I started rummaging around the area again when suddenly, the book grabbed me again! I put up a fight, but it was no use. The book was way stronger, which was surprising, considering it was just made of paper. The book had a bookmark with it and roped it around my neck, trying to choke me.

Gahh! My face turned white, then red, then about ten different shades of blue. Was this how I was going to go? Me, being torn to pieces by a wad of paper? That must be the most horrible death in the world. Well, almost.

My uncle, Persis, died after eating blue cheese. Seriously, how does that even happen?! Anyway, I'm going to be meeting my uncle soon, if I don't get free from the grasp of this book! Just then, I heard footsteps down the stairs.

Chapter 7

Why Does Vodlif Have So Many Secrets?!

(Okay, so this chapter title doesn't sound cool like the others. Sue me.)

I was dead. There was no way out of this. Unless; I dove into a box of books at the last second, just as Vodlif came in. I heard another voice. The executor!! Oh no, oh no, OH NO!!!! If Vodlif catches me in here, he'll let the executor slice my head clean off. But wait...

Vodlif reaches into a bookshelf, tugs a book, and another passageway revealed itself! Seriously, how many secrets does this man have? Anyway, I crept out of the box and followed them into the passage. The passage closed just after I went in.

 Unfortunately, the passageway closed onto my cape and ripped it. Dang! That was an expensive cape. Whatever there was no time to worry about trivial things like capes. I had to see what Vodlif was getting up to. I peeked and ducked around every corner, still trailing behind Vodlif. Suddenly, a sack was thrown over my head! The executor must've been waiting just behind the entrance!

 I heard Vodlif's voice, "What a foolish, foolish boy.", and then I heard snickering. The jokes on him because I had a PLAN. In my back pocket, I had a knife that I could use to slice through the sack. What's happening? I was being picked up and placed into what I only assume was a cart, as I could hear the wheels turning.

Suddenly there was light, and the sack was opening! Am I going to be set free? Are they going to accept a bribe?

Nope.

A ball thing was thrown into the sack with me, and then the sack was tied up again. Dang! But what was that ball? Suddenly, the ball began making whirring noises, WHIRRR.WHIRR. Until it let out a gas!! It smelt terrible, and it was making me feel a little dozy.

Oh no.

It must've been a sleep bomb! It had to be! Ooooh, I'M GONNA GET YOU VOD-

ZZZzzzz.....

Chapter 8
The Powerful

When I came to, I woke up to me being chained to a board. I tried to break free, but it was no use. Suddenly, a dark cloaked figure approached me. Was this Vodlif! That little-

"Welcome, Prince Ben."

Yep, that was his stupid, annoying voice.

"I warned you, but you wouldn't listen. Now you must pay for your actions. Oh, and don't try breaking out of those chains. They're made of videstone, the toughest substance around." Great. What could I do? Just then, Vodlif suddenly disappeared into the dark.

What was he up to?

I struggled to get out of those chains, but they wouldn't budge. It was hopeless. What do I do now? I thought up plans before thinking of ways that it wouldn't work.

Plan #1:

Use my arm strength and pull myself forward, ripping the board out of the ground along with the chains.

Problem:

I'm like a limp noodle.

Plan #2:

Whine and cry, and then make a big scene and scream, until Vodlif has had enough of me and lets me go.

Problem:

I do that even when I'm not chained up.

Rats! This is getting me nowhere. I don't have much time, and who knows what Vodlif has in store for me. Just then, I spotted something out of the corner of my eye. Was it a book? Well, that's not going to do me any good.

But wait! It looked like a magic book! Vodlif must've dropped it! And it had fallen open on a page! I could just BARELY tilt my head to see what the text says.

Chapter 9

Fire. An element. A form.

Fire is a pure form.

Harness the fire.

Embrace the fire.

BECOME the fire.

The way of fire is-

What is this baloney? "Become the fire?" Who even BELIEVES in such crap? Well, great. Now I'm really done for. As if the timing couldn't get any worse, Vodlif shows up. And he's holding a mean-looking saw. That's two things that don't mix well, Vodlif and a saw

Vodlif towers over me, holding the saw high above me.

'Harness the fire'.

'Embrace the fire.'

'Become the fire.'

"Looks like it's the end of the road for you, Benkieus."

Benkieus? Benkieus???!!!

"Don't. Call. Me. BENKIEUS!!!"

A bundle of fire explodes from my body and into a new chapter.

Chapter 10
Becoming The Fire

The wave of fire that just exploded from my body startles Vodlif, and he falls back onto his butt. The saw goes flying into the air and falls down, cutting deep into his leg. Ouch! That's going to leave a mark.

 As for the chains, they put up no fight against the fire. They melted from the intense heat, turning into mush. ("Toughest around", huh Vodlif?) I sprang off the board and dashed for the exit. However, I didn't even need to run because Vodlif groaned on the ground. He was incapacitated and couldn't lift his leg.

 So, I walked to the exit, accidentally-on-purpose stepping and squishing Vodlif's hand. He yelped out in pain, and I felt a little bad for him. YEAH, RIGHT!!

I whistled a happy tune as I walked back to the entrance, but that's when I came face-to-face with the executor.

Alright, I have enough of this guy!!

The executor didn't hesitate almost to slice my head off, swinging an axe to my head, but I reacted quickly. I ducked and then stomped on his foot. Now, he looked even MADDER. Uh oh. He took another hack at the axe, but this time I was ready for it.

With the executor on the other end, I grabbed the axe by the blade and then fire ran through my veins into my hands and through the blade and finally into the executor's hands.

They turned super red.

He screamed in pain and dropped the axe. While he was distracted, I slipped behind him and ran up the spiralling staircase that I had fallen down earlier. I then tiptoed to Dad's room. I heard snoring. Why shouldn't I even be surprised?

I can't believe he was sleeping the entire time. It was nighttime by now. What a lucky break. I then slipped into my room. Okay, that was a lot to take in. First, WHY DOES VODLIF WANT ME DEAD??! I WAS EVEN NICE TO HIM! I DIDN'T KILL HIM!

Secondly, what was that fire thing I did? Was it because of the book? Or was it because of Vodlif? Before I knew it, I fell into a deep sleep.

The following day, I woke up with dark circles under my eyes. After everything, I couldn't sleep last night. I kept having nightmares about Vodlif, the erupting, fire and axes chasing me. Oh man, I really needed some sleep. Giving up, I thought I might as well get up for the day. I managed to get out of bed, brush my teeth, and then knocked back a glass of water.

I didn't know what to do, so I watched the knights trying to avoid a piece of poop that one of the knight's horses had pooped out on the courtyard. And they were failing miserably. While I was cracking up, I went to go check on Dad.

But when I knocked on his door, no one responded. No noise came from his room.

There was no sign of Vodlif, either.

This was strange.

It seemed as if the whole castle was here, except for Dad and Vodlif.

The knights, horses, maids, chefs, gardeners, butlers, jester, Buddy (my dog), that one guy who restocks the toilet paper, and pretty much everyone else was here.

But where were Vodlif and Dad?

Chapter 11

The Portal

I went around shouting Dad's name, and even Vodlif's at one point (Only once.) I couldn't find them anywhere. I started looking everywhere, and I mean everywhere, even under the horses. I asked everyone where they were, but they also didn't have a clue.

Now, I was starting to get worried. Just then, I remembered.

The secret passage way.

YES!! THAT'S PROBABLY WHERE THEY WERE!! I HAD TO GET THERE, PRONTO! I raced down the stairs, almost cracking my anklebone, and when I came down, I stood in front of the same stuff that was there last time. There was still no sign of Dad or Vodlif.

Rats!

I kicked a box in frustration but then remembered there was another passage! I tugged on the book, which revealed the passage. I went through the hallway, hoping to find Dad or Vodlif. I was tired and in need of a sandwich. Well, only Dad.

I crossed my toes, fingers, eyes, nose, and just about every other part of my body for good luck. Annnndddd....

There was no one in sight.

NO! NO! NOOOO! WHY!! I was so done. I kicked boxes, punched the walls, and screamed in distress. I was exhausted, tired, worn out, fatigued. You get the picture. I've been going at this for a while. I really needed to find them.

I plopped down on the floor in defeat. I eyed a box of books. It seemed to stare back at me. I grabbed it, dug my hand in, and pulled out a random book. Well, I've got nothing else to do.

ucken like a skunk, it must reek to open the portal you seek, you must reek to open the portal, your kindness, like a fire, but also satire. To open the portal you seek, you must reek to open the portal, your kindness, like a fire, but also satire.

I read it aloud. What the heck is this?! Is this some sort of gibberish?! No wonder Vodlif is such a cuckoo brain. I can't even understand it! It's in English, but they're all scrambled up. I tried to decode it, but there was nothing I could do.

Open the portal...

Your kindness...

Fire...satire...

HEY! I DO NOT STINK! Stupid book...

I snapped my fingers. I've got it! I guess I must be pure of heart and be kind to open the portal. Well, that's what I'm guessing anyway. My other guess involves mustard and a unicycle.

Was I pure of heart? Definitely not; I've got a one-way ticket to Hell with my name on it, or at least Limbo. I was not going to Heaven, that's for sure. So, I wasn't expecting anything to happen, but I was surprised when the ground started rumbling.

I stood up and then got knocked over right back on my butt.

Great.

I stood up, this time hanging onto a bookshelf for balance. The ground was still rumbling and shaking like a mega-size washing machine.

What was going on?!

Just then, a portal opened.

Chapter 12
Into The Wild

My jaw dropped. I guess I was pure of heart after all? Maybe I wasn't such a bad guy. Anyways, no time to think about that now. I need to make sure I get in that portal. Dad and Vodlif are probably stuck in there! I wasn't going to take any chances.

And with that, I ran and dove through the portal. The first thing that happened was that it dropped me in mid-air, sending me crashing into a nearby pond. I looked around the world. Particles were floating in the air, in what I can only assume must be an enchanted forest.

The portal closed behind me. There was no way out of this but to go forward.

I got out of the pond. Another thing I noticed there was more anger building up inside of me. Had it been the fire? I couldn't tell. The grass was bright purple, so I knew I wasn't on Earth. Where was I?

I made my way over to the enchanted forest entrance. There, a sword lay on the grass. Something about it made it seem as though it was for me, even if it wasn't. I picked it up anyways. I was going to need to protect myself from whatever was in the forest.

My lower lip quivered because I haven't had to face danger in my entire life. It was just me stuck in the castle. I didn't even need to go out or anything and was always kept safe. My Dad would make sure.

I got a bit choked up thinking about my Dad, but I had to keep going. Wielding the sword, I entered the enchanted forest. After 15 minutes, I got attacked by a wolf with nine tails!! It was very tough, and it bit at me, tearing and ripping at my clothes. I took slashes at it with my sword. It whined and ran off. Ouch. I had bruises and cuts. I eyed a nearby pond off to the side of the trail in the forest. I crawled to it and hopped into the pond, washed my cuts, and soaking in it for a short time.

I ripped leaves and branches from trees. I tied and knotted them together to make a vest. I tore off what was left of my shirt and put the vest on. Hey, I didn't look half-bad!

I also noticed peaches in the trees, so I grabbed about five and ate two, saving the others later.

I usually don't like peaches, but at this point, I would eat a slug if I had to. After I had fueled up on the peaches, I wasn't exactly in love with the idea of going out again, but wait, what was I doing?

I HAVE POWERS!

I lit up my hand and set the sword's blade on fire.

AWESOME!

I looked so cool, with my vest and fire sword.

Anyways, there was no time for that. I continued through the forest and kept my eyes peeled for more threats. Then, I stopped short. The forest was closing to an end. I could see the other side. I could see something else.

IT WAS DAD! I raced to him and tried to hug him, but I went straight through him. He...he...wasn't here?... DANG, IT! I need someone, something, anyone to help me along the journey. Then I heard barking. I turned around. It was Buddy!

Chapter 13
Penelope

I couldn't tell you how happy I was! How did he get here? I didn't know, and I didn't care. All that mattered was that I had someone to go with. Buddy was quite a big dog, so after giving him a peach, I hitched a ride on him, and we set off.

Eventually, after walking in a big meadow and seeing much nicer animals (like see-through bunnies, but still cute), we stopped at a sign which read, "The Land of Yelk."

The Land of Yelk? Just as I thought, this place couldn't get any weirder. As we got farther down and down the trail, we came to stand in front of a huge castle. There were guards who pointed their rifles at us as soon as they saw us.

Dude!! It's a dog and a kid!! Anyway, a pretty girl came out of the entrance and told the guards to stand down. She looked about the same age as me. She was very good looking. I started blushing like a tomato field.

I wonder if...

"Hello?"

Huh? I wasn't listening at all. I was too busy looking at her and blushing like an idiot.

"I said, "Where do you come from?"

Oh! "We come from Earth; do you know what that is?"

Idiot! Of course, she knew what it is! Even an unborn child knows what that is! I'm bad at talking with girls. Luckily, she didn't look at me like I had two heads or something. She just giggled and said, "Yeah, I know what that is." She then bent down and starting petting Buddy.

Lucky dog.

"Is this your dog?"

"No, it's mine."

See what I mean?

She just giggled again. "Okay, well, would you like to come in? You and your dog seem tired."

"Yeah, I would love to go outside."

Sigh.

So, she led us to the inside of the castle, decorated with priceless treasures and expensive paintings. Wow! This was amazing; I thought, gazing on the diamond and gold chandelier hanging from the ceiling, a Chinese Ming vase that must be worth around $20 million dollars!!!!!!! (Yes, I know that that was the longest string of exclamation marks I've done, but it's $20 million!)

She looked bored and ashamed of the castle. She waved an arm at an area of famous paintings, which include Da Vinci's *Mona Lisa,* Van Gogh's *Starry Night*, and so much more!!

Yeah, I guess I'm kind of an art geek. Whatever, I just like art.

There's no way this girl could have so much stuff. She's just around the same age as me; she's got to have parents. "Do you have any parents? A Mom or a Dad?" Suddenly, all the giggling and being friendly stopped.

She just kept walking and muttered," Yeah, I guess." Dang! There goes my chances with her. When the tour was finished (which didn't seem as cool anymore), I tried to revive our little relation.

"Well, all I have to say is, "Wow, wow, wow!" Your house is incredible. I wish I had all this. Actually, not really. Buddy would try to pee in the vases."

This time, she didn't giggle. She laughed! An honest, genuine laugh.

"Thanks. And I like his name, Buddy."

Yes! She smiled. Then, just as fast as it came, the smile went away. A man with balding hair and a big belly (kind of like my Dad) stormed over to us. "Penelope, what in the world do you think you're doing, letting strangers into the house?!"

Oh no.

Chapter 14

Unexpected Guest

Yikes! Someone didn't drink their beer today. This dude was so red, and he looked like he was about to explode. What was this guy's deal? Again, it was a dog and a kid! Also, Penelope, that was her name! What a beautiful name, just like her.

(Sorry, am I ranting about her again?)

"Uncle Bill, he's not a stranger! He's my friend, my friend, Uh... what's your name?"

"Ben."

"Ben! Cool name. Anyway, he's my friend, Ben."

Hey, "friend" was better than "stranger". Maybe it will be boy-

"HE'S A STRANGER TO ME!!"

I wanted to stand up for Penelope, but this guy looked like he was about to explode! I stood there looking like a dweeb.

"Ugh, you're so annoying!"

She took my hand and raced off down a hallway, with Buddy trailing behind us. When we were out of earshot of "Uncle Bill", she said, "Sorry about that, that's just my stupid uncle, Bill. It's not you; it's him."

"That's fine; I had no idea he was such a crazy pants."

She laughed again. "You should be a jester! You're so funny!"

Please mark the date and time—May 13, 9:25 PM—because Penelope just called me FUNNY!!!!!!!!!!!!!!

(Yeah, I know, more exclamation marks. Shut up.)

Where we were standing, there were two doors on either side of us. "Alright, so do you want to have a snack before we sleep?" Aw, I wanted to stay up and just stare at Penelope until the end of time.

"No, I'm fine, goodnight."

It wasn't fine. I was starving, but of course, my idiot's brain decides to say no. Where will I sleep?

"The door behind you is the guest bedroom, and the one behind me is mine."

"Okay, sounds cool."

"Good night."

"Good night."

And with that, she kissed me on the cheek and ran into her room.

It's an excellent time to be alive.

Chapter 15

Penelope's Past

I walked into the guest bedroom and closed the door. I looked around. There was a double bed with silky sheets and a little white bathroom. I crawled under the sheets. This was amazing.

The sheets were so smooth; it felt like I was lying on a cloud! I didn't get much sleep. I just lay there thinking about Penelope, Buddy, and Dad. About everything, in general. I still didn't know my general plan.

I just jumped into the portal without thinking about what to do when I got here. It was more of a jump-and-don't-look-back kind of thing.

Just then, a scream interrupted my thoughts.

It sounded high-pitched and like Penelope! Oh no, oh no...

I swung open my door to see Penelope's door wide open, and Bill was standing over Penelope with a cleaver in his hand. WHAT THE- The SECOND Bill saw me; he dropped the cleaver and ran down the hallway, out the front door, and out of sight.

I didn't even care about Bill right now. I was more worried about Penelope. She had blood on her leg and hand marks on her throat. It didn't take a genius to know that Bill used the cleaver to hack at Penelope's leg and then tried to strangle her. The shock of everything had caused Penelope to faint, and she was now unconscious. I got down on my knees and did mouth-to-mouth. Her lips were soft and warm, and her breath smelt like honey. Maybe she should be unconscious more often.

Anyway, after about five minutes of mouth-to-mouth, she came to, gasping for air. She was alive! I tore off my vest and wrapped it around her leg to stop the bleeding. I got water and gave it to her. She couldn't move, so I carried her to bed (which probably cost more than my entire life). After a few minutes of silence, she told me the story.

"Uncle Bill was always jealous of my parents. So, when my parents passed away, Uncle Bill moved in with me because my Dad had made him my legal guardian years ago. I inherited all the money, following my parent's wishes. However, Uncle Bill was greedy and planned to assassinate me to take all the money. He probably would've gotten away with it, too, if you hadn't been here. Thank you so much."

Then she hugged me and cried on my shoulder.

Chapter 16
I Want My Mommy!

Wow. Okay. That was a lot of information to take in. It reminded me of Mom. I was about to tear up myself. No. I can't let Penelope see me acting like a wuss. So instead, I told her about my own sob story. I told her everything, from Midas to the blueberries to Vodlif, and even Dad. After I finished, she told me how sorry she was. Then, she told me to lay down with her. So, I did.

We laid down for a while in silence until Penelope cried, "I have dragon blood!" I carried her to the castle's brew room, and low and behold. She did have dragon blood! Wow, I couldn't believe it.

This time, it was in a little bag. I slipped it in my pocket, and then Penelope said, "I didn't have the chance to be with my parents, but you do. So go, I want you to have a better life than I do." She was right.

I carried her to the front door, where we said our final goodbyes. She seemed to read my mind. "Don't worry; we'll meet again, hopefully." Then, she kissed me again, but this time on the lips. She kissed me for what seemed like an eternity, but then instead of releasing me; she whispered in my ear, "Let's go to the couch."

Then, we made out. I guess this was her goodbye gift, and I loved it. And I also loved her. And her hair. And her teeth. And her-

(Sorry. Ranting again.)

Before I left, she waved at me before planting a final kiss on my right cheek. I set off, past the castle and back into the wilderness.

I think staying in a castle got me soft. When I first came into the portal, I was ready for anything. Now, I was practically scared of anything that moved or made noise. But I couldn't turn around now. Not yet anyway. I slugged through the forest, still wishing I was with Penelope.

I trekked and trekked, but nothing happened. That is until I was pulled to the ground and strangled! It was Uncle Bill! I guess he wasn't too happy that he didn't get the loot and now was mad!! My face turned five shades of blue while Uncle Bill laughed and laughed like a crazy man. (I mean, he already is a crazy man.)

I was getting sick of this guy. I grabbed at him, but he still had a firm grip on me. But I didn't die, or else you wouldn't be reading this. My leg was still free, so I kicked him right in the you-know-where. "EEEEYOOOUUUUUUUCH!" He held his groin and grimaced with pain, then laid on the ground crying like a toddler. Buddy also bit him on his butt to help.

I don't think Billy here will be trying to mess with me anytime soon. He had a small pocketknife that I took for my protection. I'm not going to kill him, so instead, I gagged him with a handkerchief and wrapped his arms in strong vines. I then dragged him into a bundle of bushes.

He's going to escape eventually, but I will be long gone by the time he does. I gave him two peaches and set them next to him. Just so, he doesn't die. I don't think anyone should be killed, even a guy like Bill. He tried to tell me something, but it came out muffled through the gag.

I didn't care anyway.

Chapter 17
Sad Ben

Even though I had Buddy with me, I still felt lonely, lost, and afraid. It was something I never felt before. I stopped to sit down and think about life. See, that's the thing. What is life? Life as we know it is utterly meaningless, but I guess God created humans for some reason. All humans have brought us pain, but some have brought affections. Like Mom, Penelope, Buddy, and yes, even Dad.

But at the end of the day, what is life about? Is it love? Is it Hate? Neither? Both? I don't have those answers, and I didn't need them. Hate – It's the cold, hard truth – and nothing else.

That's just how life is. You can't escape it. Only in one way, and it's not pretty.

It's the hard way out, but it's the only way. This was a hard thing to do. I didn't want Buddy to see and threw a stick into a bush. It would take between two and five minutes. That's all I need. I looked for a sturdy tree and grabbed a sturdy vine. I tied it around my neck, then stood on a log, and tied the other end to the tree.

Finally, I kicked the log and waited.

And waited.

And waited.

And wa-

"BEN!!!!"

That's the last thing I remember before blacking out.

Chapter 18

The Adventure Must Go On

When I woke up, I was laid on the grass, with Buddy sleeping against me. What happened? Was this Hell? Heaven? I honestly didn't know. Then I remembered everything. The tree and vine. Wow. What the Hell is wrong with me? I can't give up and take the free card! I woke up Buddy, more determined than ever, to save Dad and to reconnect with my family.

While tramping through the forest with Buddy, something occurred to me. Who called out my name? I started to get creeped out. I tried not to push the thought to the back of my mind. Just then, an old man jumped out of a bush! Buddy yelped, but I told him to stand down.

"H-Hello." I stammered. The man replied, "You look hungry and lost, young feller. I have a hut far out with resources. Let's go." I didn't have much of a choice and so followed the old man far into the trail.

We got to the hut; inside was a fire and warm food. Buddy and I walked in and sipped on the hot soup. And this point, I would eat a worm if I had to. The man leaned over and whispered, "I need sticks for a fire to warm you up. Could you lend me a hand? My bones don't work as good as they used to."

I went and got it for him. He also said to leave Buddy behind. Bit strange, but I went along with it. The area around the hut had been pretty much picked clean of sticks. I had to go deeper into the woods.

As I picked up sticks, I heard the faint sound of a dog barking. Was that Buddy? I hope not!! I had pretty much gotten a fair number of sticks. I raced back to the hut and threw open the flap. There, the old man sat next to a big pot, but WHERE WAS BUDDY????!!!

"WHAT THE HELL DID YOU DO WITH MY DOG??!!" I screamed with rage. I had fire in my eyes. I love that dog. I would die for Buddy. I asked him again," WHERE IS MY DO-"

The pot.

Oh god.

Dear Lord, please no.

I opened the pot lid.

Buddy was in there.

Dead.

Chapter 19

My "Buddy" Is Gone

Okay, this next part is going to be hard for me to write. I lost Buddy. My dog. My friend. My BEST friend. One minute he was there, barking happily, and the other, dead, in a pot. And I didn't even get to see him in his final moments.

You can probably guess what I did to the old man who had killed my dog.

No one came to the funeral.

Yes, I had KILLED someone, and I didn't even care. I was close to killing Vodlif, but even he didn't do something as wrong and terrible as KILLING my friend and dog. I cried and cried, but no one heard my weeps. I felt like dying.

I want to be there with Buddy.

But, even if I wanted to, I still must save my stupid Dad in this stupid place in this stupid world. Sigh, well, I can't rewind time. So, I slept in the hut that night and grabbed all the resources that were there. I set off again in the morning, but I didn't have my furry little sidekick this time. Life sucks.

Chapter 20

Dreams

You know, I wonder if I did all this for nothing. Like what if Dad and Vodlif aren't there? That would mean I let my dog get killed. Then again, it would've also meant that I would never have met Penelope.

I walked through this stupidly thick forest until it hit midnight. Then, I sat down, had some water before lying down and trying to sleep. It was no use. I kept tossing and turning.

I felt like someone was watching me, or something.

Eventually, I dozed off, but I kept my guard up (Kinda). I woke up, but this time, I was in my bed, in the castle. What? No, no, no. Don't tell me this whole thing was a dream. Well, most of it, I would want Buddy back.

I don't think it was a dream. I guess I was dreaming about waking up back in the castle. Yeah, confusing. To make sure it was (or wasn't) a dream, I slapped myself in the dream. Nothing happened. So, I was still in the forest, dreaming about me dreaming.

If this is a dream, then I can do anything! I knew what to do. First, I stripped down to my underwear. I don't know why, but I've always wanted to do that. Don't question it (you're probably already questioning it).

Next order of action, I went to Vodlif's room and slapped him right in the face. And again and again. CRUNCH! This is for trying to betray my Dad! KABOOM! This is for getting me in trouble! POW! And this is for being an overall annoying person (at least, I think he's human. Probably not.)

This was fun. Next, I was going to the kitchen to slather oil all over myself and slide around the castle like a penguin, but that's when I woke up. Do you know why? Because someone whispered in my ear.

SOMEONE WHISPERED IN MY EAR!

SOMEONE WHISPERED IN MY EAR!

SOMEONE WHISPERED IN MY-

I didn't get to finish that thought because, at that moment, a black figure grabbed me and put me in a headlock. I began choking. Okay, this has happened tons of times before, so I knew what to do. However, I wasn't ready for the fact this dark figure could fly! It rose, up and up and up. It zoomed through the air, still having me in a chokehold. I could see the trees, and the forest finally ended. Whatever was ahead was not much better; it was a lava pit.

Oh, so there's just a random lava pit out of nowhere. Oh, that is a bunch of baloney.

Then the imaginable happened. The figure dropped me! I went soaring through the air, screaming my lungs out, but this time, no one could help me as I went flying through the air, straight for the lava.

Luckily, the figure caught me at the last second and placed me down on the ground. It then pushed me off!

I was holding onto the edge for dear life with both my hands. The figure starts pulling off my fingers. Okay, make that one hand. Four fingers, THREE FINGERS, TWO FINGERS...

Finally, it was just my pinkie.

The figure wore a mask and then tore it off to reveal their identity.

This can't be true! It was...Penelope.

TO BE CONTINUED...

Manufactured by Amazon.ca
Bolton, ON